12-97

Merry Christmas
William
Love,
Gra   Pep-Pop

Dear Parent:

It is a fact that, at age three, children are developmentally ready to extend their social skills beyond the familiar world of their own home.

Books provide many different ways to help children socialize. For a three- or four-year-old, a book has to be read to them. So, book-reading time becomes a social time, a time for sharing. Stories first shared between adults and children can then, in turn, be shared among children. They can share impressions about what happens in the stories, or they might imitate some of the story's characters.

Jim Trelease, whose *Read-Aloud Handbook* has become a bestseller over the years, advocates making time every day for children and their families to read together. He also writes about spending less time watching T.V., because it can be an antisocial experience. A child sits alone absorbed in the visual images, but often oblivious to anything or anyone else.

Trelease writes, "A simple but boldly drawn picture book will help arouse the child's senses of sight and curiosity." *Henry's Happy Birthday* is such a book. It's a satisfying story which speaks directly to a child's experience. We think this book will make story time a happy experience for both you and your child.

Sincerely,

Fritz J. Luecke

Fritz J. Luecke
Editorial Director
Weekly Reader Book Club

Weekly Reader Children's Book Club Presents

HENRY'S HAPPY BIRTHDAY

Holly Keller

Greenwillow Books, New York

This book is a presentation of Newfield Publications, Inc.
Newfield Publications offers book clubs for children
from preschool through high school. For further
information write to: **Newfield Publications, Inc.,**
4343 Equity Drive, Columbus, Ohio 43228.

Published by arrangement with Greenwillow Books,
a division of William Morrow & Company, Inc.
Newfield Publications is a trademark
of Newfield Publications, Inc.
Weekly Reader is a federally registered trademark
of Weekly Reader Corporation.
Printed in the United States of America.

Watercolor paints and a black pen
were used for the full-color art.
The text type is Quorum Book.

First Edition
2 3 4 5 6 7 8 9 10

Library of Congress Cataloging-in-Publication Data

Keller, Holly.
Henry's happy birthday / Holly Keller.
p.   cm
Summary: Relates the disappointments and
joys of Henry's birthday party.
ISBN 0-688-09450-3.
ISBN 0-688-09451-1 (lib. bdg.)
[1. Birthdays—Fiction.] I. Title.
[DNLM: 1. Parties—Fiction.]
PZ7.K28132Hen 1990
[E]—dc20
89-23324 CIP AC

For JESSE

"Wake up, Henry," Papa whispered.
"Today is your big day."

Henry jumped out of bed and stuck his feet into his slippers. He cleared his throat and started to sing. "Happy Birthday to me, Happy Birthday to me..."

Mama was in the kitchen putting the
frosting on Henry's cake.
"Come and see," she called, when she
heard him coming down the stairs.
"You said I could have chocolate," Henry
said when he saw it.

"Vanilla will be better," said Mama, and she spread the last bit on the top. "Not everybody likes chocolate." Henry made a face. "I do," he said. "And besides, vanilla will be too plain."

Henry didn't want his cereal, so he followed
Mama into the dining room to set the table.

"Uh-oh," Mama said when she counted the candy baskets. "We forgot about Cousin Gertie. Be a good boy, Henry, and give her yours. I'll put your candy in a paper cup."

Henry picked up the shiny, silver-colored basket
and moved it slowly over to Gertie's place.
"What if you forget?" Henry said.
"Don't be silly, Henry. I won't."

When it was time to get dressed, Henry put on
his favorite T-shirt and his new sneakers.
He combed his hair and bounded back into
the dining room. "I'm ready," he announced.

"No, no," Mama said, and she laughed.
"Not today, Henry. Everyone else will be
    wearing party clothes."

Henry buttoned his white shirt, and Mama
tied his bow tie.
"There," she said. "<u>Now</u> you are ready."

"I look stupid," he said sadly.

The doorbell rang, and Henry ran to answer it.
It was Aunt Sue and Cousin Gertie.

Aunt Sue gave Henry a big birthday kiss
that left a sticky red mark on his face.

Gertie gave him a very little package
wrapped in paper Henry thought was ugly,
and he knew it couldn't be anything good.

Henry's best friend, Mark, brought a big yellow box,
but Henry could tell from the shape that it wasn't
the thing Mark had promised.
And Timmy forgot his present at home.

When everyone was there, Papa started the games.

Molly stuck a tail on Henry's back,
and Gertie called him a donkey.

The prize for musical chairs
was a little silver whistle,
and Henry wanted it.

But Timmy pushed him off the last chair just
as the music stopped. Henry was miserable.
"No more games," he said.

So Mama brought in the cake. Everyone sang "Happy Birthday," and Aunt Sue lit the candles. "One for each year and one to wish on," she said cheerfully.

Henry closed his eyes and blew. I wish, he thought, that this were someone else's birthday.
And he tried hard not to cry.

Then Papa appeared with helium balloons and
a special party hat for Henry that looked
like a crown. Everybody clapped.

Mama cut the cake and Henry got the first piece.
It was pink and white inside with real whipped cream
between the layers. Henry took a bite. It was good.
"Not too plain?" Mama asked.
Henry shook his head.

When Henry opened his presents, he got a kite
and a set of paints with a dinosaur coloring book.

Mark really did get him the crocodile raft he had promised—it just had to be blown up.

Gertie's present was a tiny model fire
engine with a siren that really worked,
and Henry loved it.

When everyone had gone home, Henry sat on Mama's lap. "Was it a nice party, after all?" Mama asked. Henry nodded his head. "But I didn't make a very good birthday wish," he said.

Mama gave him a hug. "Never mind," she said.
"You have a whole year to think of another one."
Henry smiled. "OK," he said, "I will."